EXCALIBUR

THE LEGEND OF
KING ARTHUR

Excalibur
THE LEGEND OF
king arthur

A GRAPHIC NOVEL

WRITTEN BY
TONY LEE

ILLUSTRATED, COLORED, AND LETTERED
BY SAM HART

HART
~08

CANDLEWICK PRESS

Pendragon (Pen·dra·gən) (n)
Taken from the Welsh *pen*, meaning "head" and *draeg* meaning "dragon."

In ancient times, kings of Britons would inherit the epithet *Pendragon*, which referred to their status as a "supreme war chief" or "head dragon."

The name was misinterpreted by Geoffrey of Monmouth in the *Historia Regum Britanniae* to mean "dragon's head." According to Monmouth's writings, King Uther acquired the title of Pendragon when he witnessed a dragon-shaped comet, inspiring him to display dragons on all his war standards.

LONG AGO, *LITHER PENDRAGON* WAS KING, AND THE LAND OF ALBION WAS IN DISARRAY.

FOR LITHER WAS AT WAR WITH ANOTHER: *GORLOIS*, THE *DUKE OF CORNWALL*.

GORLOIS HAD SECRETLY MARRIED *IGRAINE*, LITHER'S FIRST LOVE, AND FATHERED A CHILD, *MORGANA*.

BETRAYED, LITHER WENT TO *WAR* WITH GORLOIS – A LONG AND BLOODY ONE THAT COVERED THE WHOLE OF ALBION.

DURING THE WAR, LITHER'S NEED FOR IGRAINE WAS SO *STRONG* THAT HE DEMANDED THAT THE WIZARD *MERLIN* HELP HIM *SEE* HER.

BUT MERLIN *REFUSED*. FURIOUS, LITHER *BANISHED* HIM FROM COURT, SAYING THAT HE WOULD FIND *ANOTHER* WAY.

AND HE *DID*. HE MADE AN ALLIANCE WITH THE *UNSEELIE COURT OF FAERIE*, ASKING *THEM INSTEAD* FOR THEIR HELP IN THIS TASK.

USING THEIR *GLAMOUR*, THEIR *DARK MAGICK*, THE UNSEELIE *DISGUISED* HIM AS GORLOIS, WHILE HIS TROOPS TRICKED THE *REAL* GORLOIS OUT OF THE CASTLE.

IGRAINE BELIEVED HE WAS HER *HUSBAND*, AND AS SUCH GAVE HIM *EVERYTHING*.

AND A MILE AWAY, GORLOIS WAS *KILLED* IN BATTLE.

WITH THE WAR OVER, LITHER AND IGRAINE *MARRIED*, AND IN TIME SHE GAVE BIRTH TO A BOY . . .

ARTHUR AP LITHER—ARTHUR, SON OF LITHER, ALSO KNOWN AS *ARTHUR PENDRAGON*.

AND LITHER WAS *SCARED*.

FOR THE COST OF THE DEAL HE MADE WITH THE UNSEELIE WAS THE CHILD OF HIS MARRIAGE –*ARTHUR.*

AND SO UTHER CALLED FOR MERLIN ONCE MORE, AND MERLIN *TOOK ARTHUR* FROM UTHER, NEVER TELLING THE KING WHERE THE CHILD WOULD BE HIDDEN.

WITH ARTHUR GONE, THE UNSEELIE COURT CLAIMED THAT UTHER HAD *CHEATED* THEM.

INSTEAD THEY DEMANDED *MORGANA,* UTHER'S STEP-DAUGHTER, TO BE HANDED OVER. AND UTHER RELUCTANTLY AGREED.

BUT THE DAMAGE WAS DONE; THE *TRUST WAS BROKEN* BETWEEN UTHER AND THE UNSEELIE FAE.

IN REVENGE, THE UNSEELIE COURT TURNED TO *LORD ULRIC,* KING UTHER'S CLOSEST FRIEND AND ADVISER, CONVINCING HIM TO *ENVY* HIS KING.

THEY ENCOURAGED ULRIC'S GREED FOR UTHER'S *CROWN,* AND ULRIC FOUGHT AND *DEFEATED* HIS KING AND ONETIME FRIEND.

UTHER DIED –

– BUT NOT BEFORE *THRUSTING HIS SWORD, CALIBURN, INTO A STONE,* STOPPING ULRIC FROM *TAKING IT* FOR HIMSELF.

WITH NO UTHER TO STOP HIM, ULRIC CROWNED HIMSELF *KING OF THE BRITONS.* BUT THE WIZARD MERLIN MADE A *PROPHECY –*

– THAT ONE DAY THE SWORD WOULD BE *PULLED,* AND THE *TRUE* KING OF ALBION WOULD RULE ONCE MORE.

HE WOULD *RULE* THE PEOPLE, HE WOULD *FIGHT* FOR THE PEOPLE . . .

...AND HE WOULD *DIE* FOR THE PEOPLE.

ALBION, DURING THE REIGN OF KING ULRIC.

...DIE FOR THE PEOPLE...

ARTHUR!

ARTHUR! STOP DAYDREAMING! WE'VE GOT VISITORS APPROACHING!

I WASN'T DAYDREAMING, CEI. I WAS HAVING THAT VISION AGAIN.

THE ONE WHERE YOU'RE LYING IN THE MUD?

DAYDREAMING.

IT'S NOT A DREAM, CEI. I SEE MY DEATH. PEOPLE JUST DON'T DREAM THINGS LIKE THAT.

WHO'S COMING TO SEE US?

I'M NOT SURE. FATHER JUST SAID TO GET YOU, MAKE SURE YOU WERE THERE WHEN THEY ARRIVED.

WAIT – YOU DON'T THINK SIR ECTOR IS APPRENTICING ME, DO YOU?

DON'T EVER THINK THAT! MY FATHER LOVES YOU AS A SON!

OBVIOUSLY NOT AS MUCH AS ME, BUT THEN... I'M BRILLIANT. YOU MIGHT BE THE SON OF A KING, ARTHUR AP UTHER, BUT I HAVE STYLE AND GRACE.

AND I HAVE?

BLIND OPTIMISM AND YOUTHFUL VIGOR, WART.

THAT, AN EARNEST SCOWL, AND FAITH IN EVERYONE.

NOT *EVERYONE*, CEI. THERE'S *MERLIN*.

I LOST FAITH IN *MERLIN* YEARS AGO.

FATHER! I BRING YOU THE *ONCE AND FUTURE KING!*

OH *SHUT UP*, CEI, YOU BLOODY FOOL.

ARTHUR, I'M GLAD CEI FOUND YOU SO QUICKLY. I HAVE SOME *NEWS*, AND YOU'LL NEED TO LISTEN VERY CLOSELY.

OF COURSE, SIR ECTOR. WHAT'S UP?

WE'RE ABOUT TO HAVE VISITORS, ARTHUR. *IMPORTANT* ONES. ONES THAT YOU MIGHT NOT *WANT* TO MEET.

THEY DON'T KNOW WHO YOU *ARE*, YOU UNDERSTAND? THEY'LL THINK YOU'RE CEI'S SQUIRE. KEEP IT LIKE THAT.

YOU'RE SWEATING! WHO'S COMING?

DO YOU UNDERSTAND? YOU *CANNOT* SAY YOU'RE THE SON OF *UTHER!*

SIR ECTOR, I'VE NEVER *SEEN* YOU LIKE THIS! WHO COULD *MAKE* YOU SO?

ULRIC, ARTHUR, THE SELF-PROCLAIMED . . .

AND IT'S **KING** ULRIC, WHELP.

TEACH YOUR WARD SOME **MANNERS**, ECTOR — BEFORE HE GETS HIMSELF INTO TROUBLE.

CRACK!

AND TO WHAT DO WE OWE THIS **VISIT**, LORD KING? IT HAS BEEN **YEARS** SINCE YOU GRACED THIS HEARTH.

AYE, OVER TEN YEARS OR MORE, BY MY RECKONING. BUT FUNNILY ENOUGH, THE BOY MENTIONS THE WAY OF IT.

I'M HERE ABOUT THE **SWORD**.

EVERY YEAR SINCE I PUT DOWN THAT **RABID DOG UTHER**, THE PEOPLE OF THIS LAND GATHER TOGETHER TO TRY TO **PULL** CALIBURN FROM THE STONE.

EVERY YEAR, YOUNG MEN ARRIVE AT **STONE HILL** AND TRY TO SHOW THAT **THEY** ARE THE TRUE KING OF ALBION.

MY KINGSHIP. **MY** BRITONS. **MY** ALBION.

THIS IS AN **AFFRONT TO MY RULE**, ECTOR. **OPEN TREASON.** THEY USE THE SWORD AS A MEANS TO REPLACE ME.

NOT **THIS** YEAR. SPREAD THE WORD, LORD. TELL THEM TO KEEP AWAY THIS SPRING EQUINOX. TO RESIST IS **DEATH.**

PERHAPS IF YOU PULLED THE SWORD **YOURSELF?** THAT WAY THEY'D ALL SEE WHO'S REALLY KING!

I NEED NO **MAGIC SWORD** TO RULE THIS NATION OF FOOLS. I'VE DONE WELL ENOUGH THESE LAST TEN YEARS WITHOUT IT.

SPREAD THE WORD, ECTOR. **NO MERCY** FOR THOSE WHO IGNORE THIS DECREE.

DID YOU HEAR THAT? "DECREE." ULRIC'S LEARNED A NEW WORD.

THAT MUST HAVE TAKEN SOME DOING.

WHAT DO WE DO, FATHER?

NOTHING. EVEN IF WE TELL THEM, THE PEOPLE WILL STILL GO TO STONE HILL.

ALL WE CAN DO IS *WARN THEM* THAT ULRIC WILL BE WATCHING.

BUT FATHER! WHAT ABOUT ARTHUR? HE NEEDS TO LEARN HOW TO *DEFEND* HIMSELF IF HE'S TO BE *KING*—

HE WILL NOT LEARN SWORDPLAY WHILE UNDER MY ROOF!

I MAY HAVE OWED MERLIN ENOUGH TO TAKE ARTHUR IN, BUT I'LL BE *DAMNED* IF I HELP THAT WIZARD DRAG THE BOY TO AN EARLY GRAVE!

HE WILL HAVE TIME TO LEARN SWORDPLAY *AFTER* HE IS CROWNED! *NOT WHILE HE IS A BOY!*

NO SWORDPLAY, EH?

LOOKS LIKE IT, WART.

WE'D BETTER NOT TELL HIM WHAT YOU'VE BEEN *TEACHING* ME, THEN.

THAT *MIGHT* BE A PLAN.

CLACK!

DAMN YOU! *STAND STILL!*

CLACK!

WHAT, AND LET YOU *HIT* ME? UNLIKELY!

YOU'RE NIMBLE, FAST – BUT IN *ARMOR* YOU'LL SLOW DOWN.

AND A SWORD IS *HEAVIER*, SO YOU'LL HAVE TO COMPENSATE FOR THAT, WHEN YOU'RE KING.

SWOOSH!

NOW, COME AT ME ONCE MORE. IMAGINE YOU'RE NOT A BOY – YOU'RE *KING* ARTHUR.

CLOSE MY EYES . . . CLEAR MY MIND . . .

THE KING WOULD DIE FOR THE PEOPLE.

CLACK!

THE KING WOULD DIE FOR THE PEOPLE.

CLACK!

"*ARTHUR! STOP!*"

CEI?

OH, *THANK GOD!* IT WAS LIKE YOU WERE POSSESSED! YOU WERE GOING TO *KILL* ME!

I WOULD NEVER DO THAT. YOU'RE MY *BROTHER!*

BUT, I DIDN'T EVEN KNOW THAT I *WAS* FIGHTING YOU. ALL I SAW WAS THAT VISION AGAIN.

THAT VISION MIGHT BE *YOUR* DEATH, BUT IT WAS ALMOST *MY DEATH* THEN!

WE SHOULD STOP THIS. I KNOW YOU THINK I SHOULD KNOW HOW TO *USE* A SWORD —

— BUT I WON'T EVEN *TOUCH* CALIBURN FOR ALMOST A MONTH, LET ALONE *PULL* IT. AND WHO KNOWS WHAT'LL HAPPEN AFTER THAT!

THAT'S *EASY.* YOU'LL DEFEAT *ULRIC* AND TAKE THE *CROWN.* AND FOR THAT YOU NEED TO KNOW *HOW TO FIGHT.*

COME ON, IT'LL BE SUPPER SOON. WE CAN PRACTICE AGAIN TOMORROW.

WE STILL HAVE *THREE WEEKS* UNTIL THE EQUINOX!

YES, YOUNG ARTHUR — *PRACTICE.* IN THREE WEEKS YOU STAND AT STONE HILL.

WAR IS COMING TO ALBION, MY KING —

— AND YOU MUST BE PREPARED FOR *BATTLE.*

"DO YOU THINK THEY WILL *LISTEN*, LORD KING?"

OF *COURSE* THEY WON'T! BUT WHEN THEY *DARE* TO SHOW THEIR FACES AT STONE HILL —

— WE WILL *KILL EVERY LAST ONE* OF THEM.

WHAT I DO NOT UNDERSTAND, KING ULRIC, IS WHY THIS BOTHERS YOU *NOW?*

FOR *TEN YEARS* YOU'VE LET THEM HAVE THEIR JOUSTS, THEIR *FAYRE.* YOU'VE LET THEM HAVE THEIR FUTILE ATTEMPTS TO PULL OUT THE SWORD.

BECAUSE THIS YEAR THE SWORD IS *DESTINED* TO BE PULLED.

AND I *WILL NOT* HAVE THAT HAPPEN.

HOW DO YOU *KNOW* THIS?

WHEN I KILLED UTHER, I TOOK HIS FAMILY AS MINE. BUT HIS STEPDAUGHTER WAS *MISSING*, TAKEN FIVE YEARS EARLIER BY THE FAE.

UTHER FAILED IN A BARGAIN, YOU SEE. HE HID HIS *SON* AND GAVE HIS *STEPDAUGHTER* TO THE DARK FAE AS PAYMENT.

TEN YEARS SHE SPENT IN THE *FAERIE REALM.* WHEN SHE FINALLY RETURNED, SHE TOLD ME OF A *PROPHECY* ABOUT THE SWORD — AND ITS WIELDER.

SHE CALLS HERSELF *MORGANA LE FEY* — MORGANA OF THE FAE. SHE KNOWS THE *MAGICK* OF THE UNSEELIE COURT —

— AND SHE SAYS THAT CALIBURN *WILL* BE PULLED FREE IN *THREE WEEKS.*

CEI! WE DON'T HAVE THE *TIME* FOR THIS!

OF *COURSE* WE DO, FATHER! WE NEED TO HAVE HIM TRY THE SWORD *BEFORE* ULRIC ARRIVES!

TRY THE SWORD? YOU MEAN I'M SUPPOSED TO PULL IT NOW?

RIGHT NOW?

ULRIC'S *BOUND* TO ARRIVE AT SOME POINT TODAY —

— SO BEFORE HE COMES TO SPOIL THE PARTY, YOU NEED TO *PROVE* YOU'RE THE *ONCE AND FUTURE KING.*

"THERE'S NO BETTER TIME THAN RIGHT NOW FOR THE *SWORD IN THE STONE.*"

MAKE WAY! THIS IS THE BOY'S *FIRST TIME* WITH THE SWORD!

NEWCOMER TO THE *BLADE!*

IF MERLIN TOLD THE *TRUTH,* ARTHUR, *YOU'RE* THE ONE TO PULL THIS BLADE.

THIS IS YOUR MOMENT. THE PROPHECY STATES THAT ONLY THE *TRUE KING,* WITH THE *NEED,* CAN PULL THE BLADE.

THE LAND IS IN *TURMOIL.* ULRIC IS A *TYRANT.* WE HAVE *NEVER* NEEDED IT MORE, ARTHUR. *FREE THE BLADE. SAVE THE PEOPLE.*

THIS IS YOUR *DESTINY,* ARTHUR. THIS IS YOUR *SWORD.* HELP THE PEOPLE. PULL THE BLADE. . . .

SWISHH!

GRARGHH!!!

ARTHUR! GET *LORD LEODEGRANCE* AND HIS DAUGHTER TO SAFETY!

I'M GOING TO *HELP FATHER!* HE'S GONE UP AGAINST ULRIC!

WHACK!

ULRIC!

DAMN YOU!

SO! THE *BOY* WANTS TO PLAY AT BEING A MAN!

CEI! NO! *STAY BACK!*

HEAR ME, ULRIC OF ALBION! *THE SWORD HAS BEEN PULLED!*

TO DEMAND IT IS AN ACT OF *CHALLENGE* AND WILL BE *TREATED* AS SUCH!

MERLIN! I SHOULD HAVE KNOWN THAT THIS WOULD BE ONE OF YOUR *GAMES!* I'M NOT PLAYING!

AH, ARTHUR, SO GOOD TO SEE YOU.

AND THIS *ISN'T* A GAME, BOY. THIS IS *DEATHLY* SERIOUS.

THE BOY IS *ARTHUR PENDRAGON*, THE SON OF *UTHER* PENDRAGON, AND, AS SUCH, CLAIMS THE MANTLE OF KINGSHIP BY *HERITAGE* AND *RIGHT.*

YOU CAN CHALLENGE FOR IT TOMORROW MORNING AT *DAWN.* DO YOU ACCEPT?

AYE, I'LL RETURN TOMORROW AT DAWN. I'LL *KILL* YOUR BOY—

—AND *TAKE BACK* MY KINGDOM, WIZARD.

YAHH!

I HAVE TO FIGHT *ULRIC?* TOMORROW?

AT DAWN, YES. WON'T THAT BE *FUN?* I'M SURE YOU'RE *VERY* EXCITED—

—BUT WE HAVE A LOT TO *DO* BEFORE THEN.

WELL DONE, WART! I MEAN YOUR *MAJESTY,* WART!

MERLIN! THERE'S NO WAY THAT A FOURTEEN-YEAR-OLD BOY CAN DEFEAT ULRIC! EVEN HIS *FATHER* DIDN'T!

LET *CEI* TAKE HIS PLACE! HE HAS A BETTER CHANCE! STOP TRYING TO *CONTROL* EVERYTHING!

A BOY? LET A *MAN* FIGHT FOR HIM! YOUNG ARTHUR SAVED MY LIFE JUST THEN. ALLOW ME TO *RETURN* THE FAVOR!

YOU BOTH KNOW THE RULES OF *COMBAT BY CHALLENGE.* ARTHUR *MUST* FIGHT.

BUT TRUST ME, A *LOT* CAN HAPPEN BEFORE DAWN.

DO *YOU* TRUST ME, ARTHUR?

OF COURSE NOT! YOU STOLE ME FROM MY FAMILY AND LEFT ME ON A *DOORSTEP!*

AND ONLY AFTER LITHER *DIED* DID YOU EVEN TELL ECTOR WHO I WAS! THERE'S NOT A PERSON *ALIVE* WHO I'D TRUST *LESS!*

AND THAT'S *EXACTLY* HOW IT SHOULD BE.

HAVE NO FEAR, ECTOR. I'LL BRING HIM BACK BEFORE DAWN.

AND HE *WILL* DEFEAT ULRIC.

THIS IS **BRAN THE BLESSED,** THE RULER OF AVALON. HE HAS AGREED TO LET YOU TRAIN HERE. AND HE WILL DEBATE WITH YOU THE LAWS OF KINGSHIP.

YOU ARE WELCOME HERE, ARTHUR PENDRAGON. AS WAS YOUR MOTHER, **IGRAINE.**

YOU KNEW MY MOTHER?

OF COURSE! YOUR MOTHER WAS A **HALF FAE PRINCESS** OF THE **SEELIE COURT.**

SHE WAS ONE OF THE REASONS WHY THE **UNSEELIE COURT** WANTED YOU WHEN YOU WERE BORN.

THIS IS **BERTILAK,** THE **GREEN KNIGHT,** CHAMPION OF THE SEELIE COURT.

WITH HIS AIDES **BALAN** AND **BALIN,** HE WILL TEACH YOU THE ART OF FIGHTING.

SEELIE, UNSEELIE — WHAT DO THESE WORDS **MEAN?**

THERE ARE TWO SIDES TO FAERIE: **SEELIE** AND **UNSEELIE.** DAY AND NIGHT. SUMMER AND WINTER.

YOU LEARN FROM THE SEELIE, THE *"LIGHT"* SIDE OF FAERIE. BE VERY WARY OF THE *"DARK"* SIDE.

AND FINALLY, THIS IS **VIVIANNE,** THE **LADY OF THE LAKE.**

SHE WILL BE YOUR ADVISER, YOUR TUTOR IN THE WAYS OF **FAERIE** WHILE YOU ARE HERE.

HELLO, ARTHUR.

I — *UM,* HELLO. I MEAN . . .

WOW.

YES, SHE **HAS** THAT AFFECT ON PEOPLE.

COME ON, ARTHUR. YOU HAVE A LOT TO LEARN AND ONLY A **YEAR AND A DAY** TO DO IT IN. LET'S GET STARTED.

IT'S NOT AS IF THIS WAS A *QUICK* DECISION. EVEN THOUGH IT'S BEEN *HOURS* IN ALBION, WE'VE BEEN HERE ALMOST A *YEAR*, NOW.

I MEAN IT, MERLIN, I THINK I'M IN *LOVE* WITH HER.

VIVIANNE? SHE'S OLD ENOUGH TO BE YOUR . . .

WELL, THAT IS, SHE'S *QUITE OLD*, YOU KNOW.

I KNOW, BUT IN A WEEK I FINISH MY TRAINING AND WE RETURN. AND I MIGHT *NEVER SEE HER* AGAIN!

WHAT DO I DO? DO I *TELL* HER?

IN A WEEK WE DO INDEED RETURN, AND AT THAT POINT YOU NEED TO BE *FOCUSED.*

ADOLESCENT ACTS OF *LOVE* CAN WAIT UNTIL ULRIC IS DEFEATED.

SPOKEN LIKE A MAN WHO'S NEVER *BEEN* IN LOVE.

OH, HE'S BEEN IN LOVE, YOUNG MAN. *BELIEVE* ME.

NIMUE!

HELLO, MERLIN. I THOUGHT YOU'D GONE. I'M SO *GLADDENED* THAT YOU HAVEN'T.

CAN WE . . . MAY WE WALK *ALONE* FOR A WHILE? I'VE MISSED YOU SO.

OH, OF COURSE!

WE'LL SPEAK ABOUT THIS *LATER*, ARTHUR. YOU'RE LATE FOR YOUR SESSION WITH *BERTILAK.*

GREAT. THANKS.

FOR *NOTHING.*

DID YOU **MEAN** WHAT YOU SAID JUST THEN, ARTHUR?

THAT YOU **LOVED** ME?

WHAT? OH NO, YOU **HEARD**?

I'M TOUCHED, HONORED EVEN. BUT IT CAN **NEVER** BE.

YOU'RE A **BOY,** NOT YET SIXTEEN, AND I – WELL, I AM MUCH, **MUCH** OLDER.

AGE SHOULDN'T **MATTER!** I KNOW THAT WE COULD WORK THINGS OUT!

AND EACH DAY I GROW **OLDER,** WHILE YOU STAY THE SAME! SOON WE'LL BE **SIMILAR** IN LOOKS AND THOUGHT!

AND ON THAT DAY, I'LL **LISTEN** TO YOU ABOUT THIS. BUT CURRENTLY? YOU'RE A BOY. AND MY STUDENT.

AND BESIDES, WE BOTH KNOW THAT YOU'RE GOING TO BE A MIGHTY KING AND WILL MARRY A PRINCESS, HAVE A LONG AND HAPPY LIFE . . .

THE KING WOULD DIE FOR THE PEOPLE.

I – I KNOW.

IT'S JUST THAT – FOR **ONE** DAY . . .

. . . I WANTED TO **FORGET** MY DESTINY.

YOUNG ARTHUR, IT HAS BEEN A PLEASURE TO MEET YOU AND WATCH YOU *GROW* THIS LAST YEAR.

AND NOW, AS YOU RETURN TO YOUR *OWN* WORLD, WE HOPE THAT YOU HAVE THE STRENGTH—

—AND THE *WILL* TO DEFEAT YOUR FOE AND RESTORE ALBION TO ITS FORMER *GLORY.* DO YOU HAVE ANY FINAL WORDS BEFORE YOU LEAVE?

I'M—I'M *NOT READY,* MY LORD.

I NEED *ANOTHER YEAR.*

WHAT? ANOTHER YEAR AND A DAY? THIS *WASN'T* ASKED BY *YOU,* MERLIN!

ARTHUR, WHAT ARE YOU *DOING!* ANOTHER YEAR AND A DAY WOULD BRING US PERILOUSLY CLOSE TO ARRIVING *AFTER* THE DAWN!

AND IF WE ARRIVE TOO LATE, *WE FORFEIT THE DUEL!*

ONE MORE YEAR. ONE MORE YEAR FOR YOU TO SEE *NIMUE.*

ONE MORE YEAR FOR ME TO BE WITH *VIVIANNE* BEFORE I HAVE TO LEAVE. BEFORE I HAVE TO *GROW UP.*

STONE HILL, ALBION.

THIS IS MADNESS. CHILD OF UTHER OR NOT —

—WE CANNOT ALLOW A *BOY* TO FIGHT ULRIC! HE'LL BE *KILLED!*

AS MUCH AS I DISLIKE HIM FOR USING ME IN HIS GAMES, MERLIN IS *ALWAYS* RIGHT. IF HE HAS A PLAN THAT ENSURES A WIN —

—THEN A WIN *WILL* HAPPEN.

AND WHAT IF HE *DOES* FAIL? ULRIC HAS THE *SWORD,* AND PROCLAIMS HIMSELF THE *RIGHTFUL RULER?*

WE'LL ALL BE PUT TO DEATH! HE WON'T ALLOW US TO GO FREE!

WE NEED TO PREPARE TO *FIGHT!* TO STOP ULRIC BEFORE HE GETS TO WART — I MEAN *ARTHUR!*

I AGREE, SIR CEI! WE MUST DEFEND OURSELVES *BEFORE* ULRIC ATTACKS!

DEFEND OURSELVES *BEFORE* HE ATTACKS? ISN'T THAT CALLED "*ATTACKING FIRST*"?

YOU COULD SEE IT THAT WAY, YES! BUT WE WOULD *SECURE* ARTHUR'S THRONE BEFORE HE RETURNS!

AND THEN PERHAPS WE CAN ARRANGE A *ROYAL WEDDING, EH?* AFTER ALL, ARTHUR WILL NEED A QUEEN!

FATHER, HE MAY HAVE SAVED MY LIFE —

—BUT ARTHUR PENDRAGON IS STILL A *BOY.* . . .

IT SEEMS SO *STRANGE* THAT YOU MUST LEAVE US NOW, ARTHUR.

THAT YOU HAVE TO MOVE ON FROM US AND LIVE YOUR *REAL* LIFE ONCE MORE.

THIS IS MY REAL LIFE, VIVIANNE – AND TO LEAVE HERE, TO LEAVE *YOU* – WILL *TEAR MY HEART IN TWO.*

IN MY VISIONS I KNOW WHERE MY PATH *FINALLY LEADS.* BUT KNOW THIS, LADY OF THE LAKE.

I WILL *NEVER* LOVE ANOTHER AS I *LOVE YOU.*

AND I WILL NEVER LOVE ANOTHER AS I LOVE *YOU,* ARTHUR AP UTHER PENDRAGON OF ALBION.

YOU ARE NO LONGER A BOY. AND NOW YOU MUST GO.

THANK YOU. TO *ALL* OF YOU. WITHOUT YOUR HELP, I WOULD BE WALKING TO CERTAIN DEATH.

I JUST HOPE I *LIVE UP* TO YOUR TEACHINGS.

ARTHUR? ARE YOU ALL RIGHT?

JUST GET ME OUT OF HERE, MERLIN. I DON'T KNOW HOW LONG I CAN HOLD MYSELF STRAIGHT.

IT DOESN'T MATTER *WHAT* ULRIC DOES TODAY – WHETHER I SAVE ALBION OR NOT.

BY LEAVING VIVIANNE, I'VE *ALREADY LOST.*

...TONE HILL.

DAMN *IT!* WHERE *IS* THAT WIZARD! HE PROMISED ARTHUR WOULD BE HERE *WELL* BEFORE THE DAWN!

HE'LL *BE* HERE, FATHER. EVEN IF MERLIN'S PLANS GO AWRY, ARTHUR HAS *NEVER* LET US DOWN!

ULRIC HAS ARRIVED! HE CLAIMS THAT THE DAWN IS BUT MOMENTS AWAY —

— AND IF *ARTHUR* DOESN'T APPEAR, HE WILL CLAIM THE DUEL BY *FORFEIT!*

THEN WE MUST *FIGHT.* STRIKE HIM NOW.

WE'LL NEVER GET ANOTHER CHANCE. MERLIN. . . .

AND WHAT ABOUT MERLIN, CEI? NEVER *FORGET,* BOY —

— MERLIN AMBROSIUS *ALWAYS* KEEPS HIS WORD.

OH, I **KNEW** YOU'D TRY SOMETHING, MERLIN.

BUT IF YOU'RE GOING TO FIND A **STAND-IN**, AT LEAST FIND ONE THE RIGHT **AGE!**

I'M THE **SAME BOY** YOU TRIED TO **KILL**, ULRIC.

I JUST HAD A **GROWTH SPURT** LAST NIGHT.

LIES! I'VE HAD **ENOUGH** OF LIES! I WILL BURN **ALL** OF YOUR VILLAGES DOWN FOR THIS!

THE FIRST TIME WE MET, YOU TOLD ME HOW YOU **KILLED MY FATHER** —

— AND THEN YOU **BACK-HANDED ME TO THE FLOOR**, "**KING**" ULRIC.

OH, IT **IS** YOU. GOOD. THAT'LL MAKE THIS FIGHT LESS ONE-SIDED.

YOU MIGHT HAVE YOUR MAGICK ARMOR — BUT THAT'S **MORGANA LE FEY** BESIDE HIM.

SHE'LL HAVE USED **DARK UNSEELIE GLAMOURS** TO PREPARE HIM. BE CAREFUL.

BEWARE HIS **FAERIE-WROUGHT ARMOR**, MY KING.

IT IS **SEELIE** IN DESIGN, LIKE **CALIBURN**. IT MIGHT COUNTERACT MY UNSEELIE **SIGILS**. BE CAREFUL.

DAWN.

FOR *ALBION!*

FOR THE *KING* IS THE LAND!

YOUR LAND IS IN *WINTER,* ULRIC . . .

I AM ALBION, BOY!

...AND IT'S TIME FOR SPRING!

WAIT . . .

WAIT? IS THAT WHAT MY *FATHER* BEGGED OF YOU?

BEFORE YOU *KILLED* HIM?

PLEASE, I BEG YOU . . .

YOU *BEG* ME NOW? YOU WANT *MERCY*?

DID YOU GIVE MY *FATHER* MERCY? HAVE YOU GIVEN THE *PEOPLE OF ALBION* MERCY?

NO! YOU STRUCK HIM DOWN! YOU *KILLED* HIM!

AND NOW THE *SON* HAS RETURNED TO SEEK *REVENGE!*

THE *SWORD IN THE STONE* MUST BE *SHEATHED* ONCE MORE.

SHUNK!

YOU *LOST*, ULRIC. YIELD. YIELD TO THE *NEW KING OF THE BRITONS*.

EVEN THOUGH YOU KILLED MY FATHER, I *WON'T* KILL YOU.

GO HOME. GATHER WHAT YOU CAN CARRY AND *LEAVE* ALBION. YOU ARE *BANISHED FOREVER* FROM ITS LANDS.

THIS ISN'T *OVER*, BOY! WHEN I —

YES IT IS, ULRIC. YOU CHALLENGED AND *LOST*.

AND BY THE OLD LAWS, *ANYONE* CAN CLAIM YOUR HEAD AS A *KEEPSAKE*. I SUGGEST YOU LEAVE BEFORE *I* CHOOSE TO.

MORGANA, YOUR DARK GLAMOUR DIDN'T HELP HIM.

IN FACT, IF ANYTHING, IT *WEAKENED* HIM. WHY WOULD YOU DO SUCH A THING?

OH, MERLIN, YOU'RE SO *BLIND*. I MIGHT HATE YOU AND ARTHUR FOR WHAT YOU DID TO ME . . .

. . . BUT HE'S STILL MY *BLOOD*. AND *BLOOD* IS STRONGER THAN *ANYTHING*.

I'LL BE *SEEING* YOU, WIZARD.

SHE *HELPED* ME, DIDN'T SHE? THAT WAS MORGANA, MY HALF SISTER, WASN'T IT?

YES, IT WAS. AND YES—

—FOR SOME UNKNOWN REASON SHE DID *INDEED* ASSIST YOU TODAY. BUT BEWARE—IT'LL BE A *FAVOR* SHE'LL CLAIM BACK.

YOU MENTIONED HER IN PASSING WHILE WE WERE IN *AVALON.* YOU SAID YOU WOULD TELL ME HER STORY WHEN I WAS *READY.*

I THINK I'M READY *NOW,* MERLIN.

THEN I WILL TELL YOU IT TONIGHT. *AFTER* THE FEAST. BECAUSE THERE *WILL BE* ONE, YOU KNOW.

YOUR *MAJESTY!* I DON'T KNOW WHETHER I SHOULD *HUG YOU* OR *KNEEL!*

THE MESSENGERS HAVE BEEN SENT OUT. SOON THE *WHOLE OF ALBION* WILL KNOW WE HAVE A *NEW* KING!

AND TONIGHT WE SHALL CELEBRATE IN MY CASTLE AT *CAMELIARD!*

TOLD YOU.

MY LORD, YESTERDAY I THOUGHT YOU WERE A *BOY.* I WANTED TO APOLOGIZE....

WHY? TO YOU, YESTERDAY I *WAS* A BOY.

NOW STOP TROUBLING OUR NEW *KING,* GUINEVERE. I'M SURE YOU'LL BE SEEING EACH OTHER *MUCH MORE* IN THE FUTURE!

MAYBE EVEN IN A MORE *WEDDING-RELATED MANNER,* EH?

NOW! TO CAMELIARD! TO A *FEAST!*

"YOU WERE *UTHER'S* CHILD, AND THEREFORE HIS HEIR TO THE THRONE."

"MORGANA HOWEVER WAS A CHILD OF *GORLOIS*, AND WAS THREE OR FOUR YEARS OLDER THAN YOU WHEN THE UNSEELIE CAME."

"WITH YOU GONE, THEY CLAIMED THAT UTHER HAD *CHEATED* THEM, AND THEY DEMANDED *ANOTHER* CHILD."

"THEY DEMANDED *MORGANA*. AND UTHER RELUCTANTLY AGREED."

"FOR *TEN YEARS* SHE WAS TRAPPED THERE, LEARNING TERRIBLE THINGS AND HAVING EVEN *WORSE* THINGS HAPPEN TO HER."

"SHE TOOK *YOUR PLACE*, ARTHUR."

YOUR MOTHER, IGRAINE, WAS *HALF FAE.* AND THE UNSEELIE WANTED TO SEE WHAT WOULD HAPPEN TO SOMEONE WITH SEELIE BLOOD –

– WHEN THEY VISITED *HELL.*

MORGANA WASN'T *UTHER'S,* BUT SHE WAS STILL *IGRAINE'S.* AND SO SHE WAS TAKEN. *EXPERIMENTED* ON.

IT WAS MY FAULT. AND *THAT'S* WHY I MUST LEAVE. *THAT'S* WHY I MUST FACE MORGANA.

IF I HAD *HELPED* UTHER FROM THE START – AND CHANGED HIM AS HE ASKED – SHE WOULD NEVER HAVE BEEN TAKEN. AND YOU WOULD HAVE GROWN AS A *PRINCE.*

"AND THE UNSEELIE COURT WOULDN'T HAVE *CORRUPTED* UTHER'S CLOSEST FRIEND, *ULRIC.*"

"THEY WOULD NEVER HAVE USED HIM AS A *TOOL OF REVENGE.*"

THANK YOU FOR TELLING ME, MERLIN. ALL MY LIFE I *HATED* YOU, BELIEVING THAT YOU SIMPLY STOLE ME FROM MY FATHER FOR *PETTY REVENGE*.

BUT BEFORE YOU GO, I NEED ONE FAVOR FROM YOU.

YOU DO? WHAT IS IT, MY KING?

THEY WANT ME TO MARRY LEODEGRANCE'S DAUGHTER, *GUINEVERE*. IT'S NOT BEEN SAID YET, BUT IT WILL BE.

YET ALL I WANT IS VIVIANNE. ALL I *LOVE* IS VIVIANNE—

—AND EVERY SECOND I'M AWAY FROM HER *KILLS ME THAT LITTLE PIECE MORE*. I BEG YOU, HELP ME.

YOU KNOW WHAT YOU *ASK* OF ME? YOU'RE SURE OF THIS?

I AM. REMOVE MY MEMORIES OF MY *LOVE* FOR *THE LADY OF THE LAKE*.

LEAVE ME MY TIME IN AVALON, JUST *NOT VIVIANNE*. OTHERWISE I AM NO GOOD AS A KING TO THESE PEOPLE.

"*DREAM, MY KING.*"

"*DREAM—AND FORGET.*"

STATE YOUR NAME AND PURPOSE!

I AM SIMPLY *MERLIN*, GOOD MAN. AND I AM HERE TO SEE THE LADY MORGANA.

IF YOU COULD TELL HER . . .

NO NEED. SHE'S BEEN *EXPECTING* YOU.

SHE HAS?

MY LADY MORGANA . . .

AH, MERLIN, *THERE* YOU ARE.

YOU'RE *HALF AN HOUR LATE.*

OW. THAT *HURT.*

DAMN YOU, MORGANA.

SNOW? BUT IT WAS *SPRINGTIME!*

WHERE HAVE YOU SENT ME, WITCH?

HO THERE! *YOU, SIR!*

HELP A MAN IN DISTRESS? PLEASE?

BLOW ME! *MERLIN THE MAGICIAN!* I THOUGHT YOU WERE DEAD!

I ALMOST WAS.

WAIT – YOU *KNOW* ME? WHERE AM I?

WHERE *ARE* YOU? WHY, YOU'RE IN THE KINGDOM OF ALBION, NEXT TO THE MIGHTY *CAMELOT ITSELF!*

CAMELOT? IT CAN'T BE. ARTHUR HAD ONLY JUST STARTED TO *TALK* ABOUT SUCH A CASTLE!

AYE, HE TALKED FOR ABOUT A YEAR, AND THEN IT TOOK ANOTHER *THREE* TO BUILD.

BUT FOR THE LAST *THREE YEARS* HE'S LIVED THERE —

— *KING ARTHUR OF CAMELOT.*

...*SEVEN* YEARS?

PLEASE, TELL ME, WHAT *ELSE* HAS HAPPENED IN THE LAST SEVEN YEARS?

THINGS OF NOTE? WARS? *WEDDINGS?*

WELL THERE WAS THE *WEDDING,* OF COURSE! HE MARRIED *GUINEVERE,* DIDN'T HE!

IT WAS A BEAUTIFUL DAY. EVEN THE *FAERIE FOLK* CAME TO SEE IT!

HE ALSO MET THE GREAT KNIGHT *LANCELOT.* THEY FOUGHT, AND THEN KING ARTHUR MADE LANCELOT HIS *CHAMPION.*

SO HE FINALLY BECAME THE KING HE *WANTED* TO BE, EH?

AYE, AND *MORE.* KING ARTHUR HAS *UNIFIED THE LANDS,* BROUGHT THE WARRING TRIBES UNDER *ONE RULE.*

FOR THE FIRST TIME IN YEARS WE HAVE *FOOD TO SPARE,* WE FEEL *SAFE* IN OUR HOMES, AND WE KNOW WHAT *HOPE* IS.

ARTHUR SAVED US ALL. ALL OF ALBION *LOVES* HIM.

DOES THAT HELP YOU, MY LORD?

IN A WAY, YES. THANK YOU.

NOW, IF YOU'LL EXCUSE ME — I HAVE A *KING* TO VISIT.

MY KING, I CAN'T EXPLAIN *WHERE* I'VE BEEN.

IT DOESN'T MATTER. YOU'RE HERE NOW.

NO, MY LORD. I MEAN THAT A MATTER OF *HOURS* AGO FOR ME, IT WAS *SEVEN YEARS AGO* FOR YOU!

MORGANA *WON* THE FIGHT AND TRANSPORTED ME HERE.

WELL, THEN YOU HAVE A LOT TO CATCH UP ON!

YOU REMEMBER MY FOSTER FATHER, ECTOR, AND BROTHER, CEI?

IT'S GOOD TO SEE YOU, MERLIN! YOU COULDN'T HAVE TIMED IT BETTER!

YOU MEAN MY *WIFE!* GUINEVERE AND I MARRIED *FIVE YEARS AGO!*

WHERE'S LEODEGRANCE AND HIS DAUGHTER?

SHE'S ATTENDING TO HER FATHER AT CAMELIARD. HE BROKE HIS LEG IN A TOURNEY A COUPLE OF MONTHS AGO.

COME, MERLIN! I HAVE SOMETHING TO SHOW YOU!

OH, ARTHUR. YOU FOUND LOVE –

– BY FORGETTING YOUR *TRUE* LOVE.

THE *ROUND TABLE!* NOW ALL MY KNIGHTS AND ADVISERS ARE *EQUAL.* NO MORE SHOUTING DOWN LONG TABLES. IT WAS LEODEGRANCE'S IDEA.

A FINE IDEA, ARTHUR. WHO...?

OH, IT WAS A PRESENT FROM THE *LADY OF THE LAKE.* IT WAS BROUGHT TO ME BY HER *NEPHEW* WHEN HE CAME TO JOIN US.

IT'S STRANGE THOUGH. I SEEM TO REMEMBER *MEETING* HER BACK IN AVALON, BUT I CAN'T PLACE HER FACE....

NEPHEW?

FOSTER NEPHEW, ACTUALLY. LIKE ME. HE'S BEEN HERE *TWO YEARS* NOW, AND HE'S THE *KING'S CHAMPION.* HE FIGHTS FOR ME WHEN I CAN'T TAKE SIDES. HE IS MY GREATEST DIPLOMAT.

MERLIN AMBROSIUS —

— MEET *LANCELOT DU LAC!*

IT IS A PLEASURE TO FINALLY MEET YOU, MY LORD.

MY ADOPTED AUNT HAS SPOKEN MUCH OF YOU. AS HAS THE LADY NIMUE.

YOU KNOW VIVIANNE? YOU KNOW NIMUE?

OF *COURSE* HE DOES. HE'S HALF FAERIE TOO. HE WAS ALSO TAUGHT HOW TO FIGHT BY BERTILAK!

MY PARENTS WERE *KING BAN AND QUEEN ELAINE OF BENWICK,* ACROSS THE SEA.

MY MOTHER IS *SISTER* TO THE LADY VIVIANNE AND FOR MUCH OF MY CHILDHOOD I STAYED IN AVALON.

MY ADOPTED AUNT WAS **CONCERNED** ABOUT ARTHUR, AND WISHED ME TO ATTEND HIM.

I HAD BEEN TRAINED THROUGHOUT MY LIFE TO BE THE **BEST THAT I COULD BE**, AND VIVIANNE BELIEVED THAT THIS WAS NEEDED BY ARTHUR.

OF **COURSE**, HE DECIDED THAT THE **BEST** WAY TO ATTEND ME WAS TO **CHALLENGE** ME!

FOUR HOURS WE FOUGHT – UNTIL HE SIMPLY STOPPED, KNELT BEFORE ME, AND SWORE TO MY SWORD.

LANCELOT, MY FRIEND, TAKE SOME MEN TO CAMELIARD AND ESCORT THE QUEEN BACK HERE. WE SHALL HAVE A **FEAST!**

YES, MY KING.

REMEMBER TO TAKE **CALIBURN.** YOU ARE THE KING'S CHAMPION AFTER ALL!

LANCELOT HAS ONLY BEEN HERE TWO YEARS, BUT ALREADY HE IS MY CLOSEST FRIEND. AND GUINEVERE'S TOO.

YOU LET HIM TAKE CALIBURN? I THOUGHT THAT ONLY **YOU** – ONLY A MAN **PURE OF HEART AND SOUL** – COULD WIELD IT?

IT'S TRUE, BUT HIS **LINEAGE AND HIS TUTORSHIP** ALLOWS HIM TO WIELD CALIBURN, WHILE PURE OF HEART.

AND I CAN'T SEE **THAT** CHANGING FOR A WHILE. AFTER ALL, THIS IS **CAMELOT....**

"...WHAT COULD **POSSIBLY** CORRUPT HIM HERE?"

AH, THE **MIGHTY** LANCELOT—

—WE'VE BEEN **WAITING** FOR YOU.

WE BRING NEWS FROM YOUR **FAMILY.**

I **HAVE** NO FAMILY IN THE **UNSEELIE COURT.**

AH YES, YOU'VE GONE ALL **SEELIE** ON US, HAVEN'T YOU.

LANCELOT "**OF THE LAKE,**" INDEED.

YOUR ADOPTED FAMILY MIGHT BE ALL **SUNSHINE AND RAINBOWS,** LANCELOT—

—BUT YOUR ORIGIN IS SET IN STONE. **ARCADIAN** STONE.

WATCH CAREFULLY WHAT WORDS YOU SPEAK NEXT, FAE—

—MY PARENTS WERE BOTH MORTAL AND SEELIE. **YOUR** COURT HAS NO SAY HERE.

DO NOT TRY TO **LIE** TO US, KNIGHT. WE KNOW EVERYTHING, EVEN IF **YOU** DON'T.

YOUR MOTHER WAS **UNSEELIE.**

EXCELLENT. THE OFFER HAS BEEN MADE. AND THE TRAP HAS BEEN SET.

HE CAN'T ESCAPE HIS LOVE FOR THAT SIMPERING *GUINEVERE* BUT IT WILL *DESTROY* HIM.

AND IN DOING SO, HE WILL DESTROY *CALIBURN,* *CAMELOT,* AND *ARTHUR.*

DO YOU HAVE PROOF? THAT HE *LIVES?*

YES, MY LADY *MORGANA.* IT IS CONFIRMED. MERLIN HAS RETURNED TO CAMELOT.

I WAS CERTAIN HE WAS DEAD, BUT IT SEEMS EVEN AN *OLD* DOG CAN LEARN NEW TRICKS.

STILL, MUSTN'T DWELL ON THE *PAST.* TODAY IS ABOUT THE FUTURE.

GIVE *MALEAGANT* THE ORDER TO TAKE GUINEVERE FROM HER FATHER'S HOME.

TELL HIM TO BRING HER TO THE *KILLING TREES* AND *WAIT.*

IF LANCELOT WON'T PURSUE HIS DESTINY –

– THEN WE'LL SIMPLY HAVE TO *BRING IT TO HIM.*

SMILE, LANCELOT. MERLIN'S BACK! IT'S A TIME FOR GREAT CHANGE!

I NEVER KNEW MERLIN, *BEDIVERE*, SO I HAVE NO NEED TO BE *CHEERFUL* OF HIS RETURN.

BESIDES, WHEN HE LOOKED AT ME, I FELT A *CHILL* SHIVER DOWN MY SPINE.

HE DOES THAT TO EVERYONE. I REMEMBER A TIME AT STONE HILL —

GAWAIN, *GAWAIN.* YOU MET HIM ONCE. AND YOU WERE *TEN!*

DON'T TRY TO PLAY US LIKE CHILDREN!

HE SAID I HAD A *GREAT FUTURE* AHEAD OF ME.

HE DIDN'T MENTION IT'D INVOLVE *BULL-HEADED IDIOTS* LIKE YOU.

LOOK! WHAT'S THAT?

WHERE? WHAT ARE YOU —

— OH, *NO.*

IT'S LEODEGRANCE. SOMEONE'S TORCHED *CAMELIARD.*

LORD *LEODEGRANCE!* WHAT HAPPENED?

THEY *TOOK* HER! THEY TOOK *GUINEVERE.* SHE'S GONE!

IT WAS *MALEAGANT.* HE HAD AN ARMY OF SOLDIERS!

WE WEREN'T PREPARED. THEY TOOK US APART! THE MAIN FORCE THEN WENT SOUTH —

— BUT MALEAGANT AND SOME MEN TOOK HER *EASTWARD.*

MY REMAINING MEN WENT AFTER THEM, BUT WERE CUT DOWN.

THEY'RE HEADING TOWARD THE *KILLING TREES!*

NO! HE **CAN'T** BE SERIOUS!

WHAT ARE THE KILLING TREES? WHY WOULD HE GO THERE WITHOUT HIS MEN?

IT'S A MESSAGE TO ARTHUR. AND HE **WON'T** BE STAYING THERE LONG.

YEARS AGO, MALEAGANT WAS ULRIC'S **STEWARD.** HE TOOK HIS MASTER'S LOSS PERSONALLY.

ULRIC USED TO TAKE TRAITORS TO THE CROWN TO THE KILLING TREES, WHERE HE WOULD **HANG THEM**

AND THAT'S WHERE MALEAGANT'S TAKEN GUINEVERE. WHAT DO **YOU** THINK HE INTENDS TO DO?

YOU'RE MAKING A BIG MISTAKE HERE. WHEN MY *HUSBAND* HEARS OF THIS –

HE WILL COME FOR US ALL. NO STONE WILL BE UNTURNED. YES, I'VE HEARD IT *ALL* BEFORE.

BUT YOU'LL STILL BE *DEAD*, MY LADY. THE *MESSAGE* WILL BE SENT.

YOUR PRETENDER HUSBAND NEEDS TO BE TAUGHT THAT *SOME* PEOPLE WANT IT BACK THE WAY IT WAS. AND WILL DO *ANYTHING* TO MAKE IT SO.

NOW. BRING HER HERE.

THEY'RE GOING TO *HANG* HER! WE HAVE TO DO SOMETHING!

IT'S TWO-TO-ONE ODDS. ARE WE HAPPY WITH THAT?

TOTALLY.

WHAT THE –

DIIEE!!!

LANCELOT! SAVE GUINEVERE!

FOR ARTHUR!

ABOUT TIME, TOO. I THOUGHT YOU WERE NEVER GOING TO GET HERE.

CLANG!

MALEAGANT IS UNFORTUNATELY **DEAD IN A DITCH** IN KENT. BUT WE FELT HIS **APPEARANCE** WAS VITAL.

THE UNSEELIE COURT IS ALL ABOUT THE **STORY**, YOU SEE. **ARTHUR'S** STORY.

I'LL SEE YOU IN **SPRING**, COUSIN.

STRIKE TRUE. BECOME THE **LEGEND**. FOLLOW THE TALE TO THE END.

DIIIIIEEEEEE!!!!

GLAMOUR.

NOTHING BUT **GLAMOUR** AND A **RUSTY BLADE**.

LANCELOT?

CAMELOT.

GUINEVERE! WHAT HAPPENED?

MY FATHER WAS ATTACKED! WE NEED TO SEND AID IMMEDIATELY!

IF IT WASN'T FOR *LANCELOT*...

IF IT WASN'T FOR *ALL* OF US, MY LADY.

MALEAGANT KIDNAPPED THE QUEEN, MY KING. WE TOOK HER BACK.

YOU ARE *TRULY* MY BROTHER! COME, LET ME ARMOR UP! LET US *PUNISH* THE MISCREANT KNIGHT!

THERE IS NO NEED, MY LORD. I *KILLED* HIM.

BUT SIR BEVIS FELL TO AN ARROW.

THEN WE SHALL HOLD A *FEAST* TONIGHT IN HIS HONOR!

AND TO CELEBRATE MY QUEEN'S RETURN — AND MALEAGANT'S DEATH!

MALEAGANT? IT *LOOKED* LIKE HIM, BUT AT THE END I SWEAR I SAW—

IT WAS *MALEAGANT!* NOTHING MORE! JUST A MAN! DO YOU *DOUBT MY WORD?*

NO, IT'S JUST...

THEN THIS CONVERSATION IS *OVER!*

MY LADY? ARE YOU ALL RIGHT?

YES. IT'S SILLY OF ME, REALLY. TO BE *JEALOUS* OF YOU MARRYING SOMEONE —

— WHILE *I* AM MARRIED TO SOMEONE ELSE.

JUST PROMISE ME THAT *WHEN* YOU MARRY —

— YOU MARRY FOR *LOVE*, OR NOT AT ALL.

GUINEVERE, YOU'RE CRYING!

MY QUEEN — I CAN'T HONOR THAT REQUEST BECAUSE —

— BECAUSE I *ALREADY* LOVE SOMEONE, AND I CAN *NEVER* MARRY HER.

PLEASE, LANCELOT, DON'T SAY ANYTHING ELSE —

— YOUR PURITY IS YOUR *STRENGTH*. TO SAY WHAT YOU THINK—

WOULD BE A *RELIEF*. AND IF SAYING THIS MEANS THAT I AM NO LONGER PURE? THEN SO BE IT.

I LOVE YOU, GUINEVERE. I HAVE, DO NOW, AND ALWAYS WILL.

LANCELOT, I'VE BEEN SO LONELY . . .

LOOK AT HIM. PLUMMETING HAPPILY TO HIS DOOM. *DAMNING* CAMELOT AND HIS KING WITH A *KISS.*

IS *THIS* WHY YOU BROUGHT ME BACK TO ALBION, MORGANA? TRICKS AND LIES?

IS *THIS* WHY I STAND IN A FAERIE REALM, *STILL NOT KING?*

SHUT UP, *ULRIC.* YOUR DAYS AS KING ARE OVER, BUT YOU STILL HAVE A *PART* TO PLAY.

ARROGANT WITCH! I SHOULD HAVE TAUGHT YOU MANNERS WHEN I –

I WAS TAUGHT *"MANNERS"* BY A FORCE *FAR WORSE* THAN YOU, STEPFATHER.

NOW. YOU CAN EITHER TAKE YOUR PLACE AT MY SIDE, OR I CAN *KILL YOU* WHERE YOU STAND.

ACK – I –*ALL RIGHT!*

– GASP –

SO WHAT'S NEXT? WE PLAY WITH THE PRETTY BOY KNIGHT SOME MORE?

NO, THAT'S TOO SIMPLE, TOO FAST.

I WANT TO HURT ARTHUR ON A *LONG-TERM* BASIS.

IT'S TIME FOR ARTHUR TO HAVE A MIDNIGHT VISITOR. HIS *TRUE* LOVE.

IT'S TIME FOR *FAERIE GLAMOUR* TO COME OUT AND PLAY.

ARTHUR'S CHAMBERS.

HRR — NO . . .

WHA — WHO'S THAT?

GUINEVERE? IS THAT YOU?

IT IS I, ARTHUR.

YOUR *TRUE* LOVE.

VIVIANNE? WHAT ARE YOU — NO, *STOP* — GET OFF —

WHY DO YOU STOP ME? YOU *LOVE* ME. YOU *WANT* ME. YOU CREATED THIS *GLAMOUR* OF ME.

ACCEPT ME. TAKE ME IN YOUR ARMS.

LOVE ME.

AND THEN THEY DISCOVER THAT SHE'S ONLY A *HAG* DURING THE DAY!

I STILL THINK IT NEEDS MORE WORK, *TALLIESIN.*

HELP... ME...

PLEASE... MERLIN...

ARTHUR!

QUICK! *GET MERLIN!*

THUD!

STAY WITH ME, ARTHUR! WHO DID THIS?

WHO DID THIS?

A MONTH LATER.

HOW ARE YOU FEELING TODAY, MY KING?

BETTER. STRONGER. NOT AS STRONG AS I WAS—

—BUT SLOWLY, DAY BY DAY, I GET THERE.

THE EMISSARY FROM *AVALON* RETURNED. BRAN STILL WON'T ACCEPT YOUR APOLOGY.

AND APPARENTLY *THE GREEN KNIGHT* HAS GONE MISSING.

I DON'T BLAME HIM. I WOULDN'T HAVE, EITHER. IT WAS JUST—WELL, VIVIANNE—

—IT WAS *HER*, MERLIN. SHE FELT SO *REAL*.

FOR YEARS I'VE FELT *HOLLOW*, AS IF *MISSING* SOMETHING. I THOUGHT IT WAS THE LOSS OF YOU, BUT WHEN YOU RETURNED IT WAS STILL THERE.

AND WHEN VIVIANNE—OR WHATEVER IT WAS—APPEARED, SUDDENLY I WAS *COMPLETE*. AND THEN IT WAS GONE AGAIN.

IT'S ALMOST LIKE I *LOST* SOMETHING, BUT DON'T REMEMBER WHAT IT WAS.

A VEIL HAS BEEN PULLED TO THE SIDE. I *LOVE* GUINEVERE, BUT THERE WAS *SOMEONE ELSE*, WASN'T THERE? SOMEONE I'VE FORGOTTEN?

THERE WAS, AND IT *WAS* VIVIANNE. YOU FELL IN LOVE IN AVALON.

BUT YOU KNEW THAT TO *RULE* ALBION, YOU WOULD EVENTUALLY HAVE TO MARRY *ANOTHER*, AND SO YOU BEGGED ME TO REMOVE YOUR *MEMORIES* OF HER.

SHE BECAME NOTHING MORE THAN A STRAY THOUGHT.

I—I THINK I REMEMBER. THIS HAPPENED THE NIGHT YOU LEFT!

BUT WHY DO YOU TELL ME *NOW*?

WHERE ON *EARTH* ARE GUINEVERE AND LANCELOT?

I SENT HIM TO FIND HER OVER *HALF AN HOUR* AGO!

I'VE NO IDEA, ARTHUR. PERHAPS HE GOT LOST?

DOUBTFUL. THE AMOUNT OF TIMES HE'S ESCORTED HER TO HER QUARTERS, HE'D KNOW THE ROUTE BETTER THAN TO HIS OWN.

PERHAPS I SHOULD —

ARTHUR!

CRASH

ARTHUR PENDRAGON! THE BOY WHO BECAME KING!

THE *LIAR* MORE LIKELY! THE STEALER AND *DESTROYER* OF HEARTS!

SIR BERTILAK, I HAVE BEEN WORRIED ABOUT YOU.

I HEARD THAT YOU HAD GONE MISSING FROM AVALON.

I CARE NOT ABOUT YOUR *WORRY!* I DEMAND RECOMPENSE FOR THE LADY OF THE LAKE'S *HONOR!*

HONOR THAT *YOU* DEFILED!

ARTHUR DIDN'T DEFILE VIVIANNE! *SHE* WAS THE ONE WHO CAME TO HIS BED!

NO, CEI, THAT WAS A CREATURE OF *GLAMOUR*, MADE TO LOOK LIKE HER.

SHE IS A *WRONGED PARTY*, AND BERTILAK HAS A *RIGHT* TO JUSTICE.

WHAT DO YOU WANT, BERTILAK? WHAT DOES *VIVIANNE* WANT?

FOR HOW ARTHUR *TREATED* HER WHEN SHE OFFERED HIM A *CURE*, I WANT HIS *HEAD*, MERLIN.

SHE WANTS NOTHING. SHE KNOWS IT WAS AN UNSEELIE GAME. BUT THAT IS *NOT THE POINT!*

I SEE YOU'RE STILL NOT WELL ENOUGH TO *FIGHT*. AND YOUR *CHAMPION* SEEMS TO BE MISSING.

SO INSTEAD, I CHALLENGE YOU TO A *CONTEST*.

VERY WELL.

NO, MY LORD, YOU **WILL NOT** PLAY THESE FAERIE GAMES!

IF SOMEONE NEEDS TO BE THE GREEN KNIGHT'S **PLAYTHING**, THEN IT SHALL BE ME!

TELL ME THE RULES, SIR BERTILAK. WHAT GAME DO WE PLAY?

IT IS A SIMPLE ONE, SIR GAWAIN. EVEN **YOU** CAN PLAY THIS ONE.

YOU JUST HAVE TO **CUT OFF MY HEAD.**

IF I SURVIVE, I CUT YOURS OFF IN A **YEAR AND A DAY**. A FINE LENGTH OF TIME. IN FACT, THE **SAME** AGREEMENT ARTHUR MADE IN **AVALON.**

YOU'RE **INSANE!** YOU WON'T SURVIVE! AT THIS RANGE I CAN'T MISS!

THEN IT WILL PROVE THAT ARTHUR IS **JUST** IN HIS ACTIONS, AND HONOR WILL BE RETURNED.

STRIKE, KNIGHT. OR ARE YOU TOO **SCARED?**

NEVER.

SHUNK

CLATTER!

A FINE BLOW, SIR GAWAIN.

BUT IT LOOKS LIKE *MY* CAUSE IS *TRUE*, DOESN'T IT?

IN A *YEAR AND A DAY*, ARTHUR, I WILL RETURN AND TAKE MY SWING AT SIR GAWAIN'S HEAD, AS HE TOOK YOUR PLACE.

IF THE AX FALLS AND *DOESN'T* CUT HIS HEAD OFF? THEN I WILL AGREE THAT MY LADY'S *HONOR* IS RETURNED. IF NOT —

— JUST REMEMBER THAT WHATEVER HAPPENS, IT IS *YOUR FAULT*, KING ARTHUR.

EVERY LAST PIECE OF IT.

SEE YOU IN A *YEAR AND A DAY*, MORTAL.

ARE YOU ALL RIGHT?

BLOODY *FAERIE GAMES!* THAT'S ALL THIS WAS!

HOW DO I RETURN THE FAVOR IN A YEAR? MY HEAD WON'T DO WHAT *HIS* DID!

WELL, THE *BAD* NEWS IS THAT A YEAR FOR BERTILAK IS ONLY A DAY FOR YOU—

—SO EXPECT HIM BACK AFTER DAWN TOMORROW.

THE *GOOD* NEWS IS THAT IT'LL ALL BE OVER SOON, THOUGH!

FAERIES! LANCELOT SHOULD HAVE BEEN HERE FOR THIS! THIS WAS *HIS* FIGHT, NOT MINE!

I'M SO GLAD TO SEE THAT YOU FIND THIS *FUNNY,* WIZARD!

OH, COME ON, ARTHUR— BERTILAK WON'T CUT OFF GAWAIN'S HEAD.

HE WANTS TO CUT OFF *YOURS.*

IT'S JUST A SHAME YOUR *CHAMPION* WASN'T HERE. I WONDER WHERE HE IS?

YOU AND ME BOTH. WHEREVER HE IS . . .

"...HE'D BETTER HAVE A *DAMNED GOOD REASON* FOR HIS DELAY!"

WE'RE SO LATE! THEY'LL BE WAITING FOR US!

IT'S A *ROYAL FEAST.* WITH THE AMOUNT OF PEOPLE IN THE HALL, THEY WON'T EVEN HAVE NOTICED THAT WE AREN'T THERE.

OF COURSE, I MIGHT BE *WRONG.*

HO, GAWAIN! WE WERE JUST COMING!

I'VE BEEN *LOOKING* FOR YOU, *CHAMPION.* YOU'RE WANTED AT COURT.

BUT I SHOULD HAVE GUESSED YOU'D BE *PICKING FLOWERS* – WITH *HER.*

THAT *"HER"* IS THE QUEEN OF –

I DON'T WANT TO HEAR WHAT YOU HAVE TO *SAY,* LANCELOT!

YOUR KING *NEEDED* YOU, *AND YOU WEREN'T THERE!*

ARTHUR IS IN TROUBLE?

WAS. LUCKILY HE STILL HAD A COUPLE OF LOYAL KNIGHTS WHO KNEW WHAT THEIR *PRIORITIES* WERE.

I TOOK AN *AX-SWING* FOR YOU TODAY.

YOU CAN TAKE THE *NEXT ONE.*

EITHER OF YOU. I DON'T CARE ANY MORE.

I FOUND YOUR MISSING CHAMPION, MY LORD.

MY KING, I AM *SORRY* FOR OUR DELAY.

THE QUEEN WAS FEELING UNWELL AND I HAD TO WAIT FOR HER. BUT GAWAIN'S WORDS –

THE FEAST HAS *ENDED*, MY QUEEN. WHICH MEANS THAT YOU'RE NOT LATE – YOU WERE *ABSENT ENTIRELY*.

AND IF *EITHER* OF YOU HAVE AN ISSUE WITH GAWAIN, WHO TOOK LANCELOT'S PLACE TONIGHT IN MY *DEFENSE* –

– THEN YOU SPEAK TO *HIM*. WORK OUT YOUR ISSUES.

I'LL DO BETTER THAN THAT, MY KING! I *CHALLENGE* LANCELOT!

I'VE HAD *ENOUGH* OF THEIR LIES! *LANCELOT AND HIS QUEEN LOVER!* DO YOU THINK WE HADN'T *NOTICED?*

I SAW YOU AT THE *CARAVAN!* WE'VE SEEN YOU IN THE *GARDEN!*

THERE'S NOT A *KNIGHT IN CAMELOT* WHO DOESN'T KNOW OF YOUR SECRET! YOU MAKE A *MOCKERY* OF THE MARRIAGE –

OH, TRUST ME, GAWAIN, *THAT* ISN'T A MOCKERY OF THEIR MARRIAGE –

– BUT I'M ABOUT TO SHOW YOU SOMETHING THAT *IS*.

HELLO, *BROTHER.*

MORGANA! HOW DARE YOU APPEAR HERE! YOU'RE *BANISHED* FROM ALBION!

OH, MERLIN, YOU ALWAYS THINK SO *LITERALLY!*

SO *SMALL* OF THOUGHT!

A MONTH AGO I SENT YOU A *VISITATION*, BROTHER – A CREATURE OF GLAMOUR – TO STEAL YOUR VERY *ESSENCE!*

IT TOOK THE FORM OF THE ONE YOU *LOVE THE MOST!*

BUT YOU – YOU SAW *VIVIANNE!*

YOU *LIE*, MORGANA! STOP YOUR TRICKERY AND TELL ME WHY YOU'RE HERE!

I COME TO SHOW THIS! THE *RESULT* OF THE VISITATION!

A CHILD *EXACT IN EVERY WAY* TO YOU!

I SHOW YOU *MORDRED PENDRAGON!*

YOU HAVE A *SON*, ARTHUR.

OUR WAR HAS BEGUN.

AND IN YOUR FINAL BATTLE HE WILL *DESTROY* YOU.

FAERIE GAMES.

LANCELOT, GAWAIN, YOU FINISH THIS *TOMORROW.* ONE OF YOU WILL BE VINDICATED . . .

TODAY WE SETTLE AN ARGUMENT BETWEEN TWO OF ARTHUR'S FINEST KNIGHTS: *GAWAIN* AND *LANCELOT.*

GAWAIN ACCUSES LANCELOT OF *ADULTERY,* OF FALLING FROM GRACE. AND LANCELOT *DENIES* THESE CLAIMS.

THEY HAVE DECIDED ON *TRIAL BY COMBAT* TO PROVE WHOSE WORD IS TRUE.

IF THIS FIGHT ENDS AND YOU ARE PROVEN *LIAR?* FOR WHAT YOU HAVE SAID ABOUT MY DAUGHTER —

— I WILL *CUT OUT YOUR SPLEEN* WITH A CUTLERY KNIFE.

AND YOU — IF YOU PROVE TO BE A *FALSE* KNIGHT —

— I'LL LEAVE YOU TO *ARTHUR.* AND IT'LL BE *WORSE.*

FIGHT!

I DON'T WANT TO *FIGHT* YOU, GAWAIN. YOU'RE MY BROTHER KNIGHT—

I'M NO BROTHER TO *ADULTEROUS SCUM* LIKE YOU! YOU'VE BROKEN THE CIRCLE! *DOOMED US ALL!*

AND THAT HARLOT IS NO *QUEEN OF MINE!*

NEVER CALL GUINEVERE THAT!

IT'S TRUE. I'VE *DOOMED CAMELOT.*

I HAVE *FALLEN FROM GRACE,* JUST LIKE THEY SAID.

I AM NO LONGER PURE OF HEART, MY LORD!

BUT GUINEVERE IS *BLAMELESS* IN THIS! IT WAS MY FAULT! *SPARE HER!*

IT WAS TRUE? YOU AND *LANCELOT?*

I *LOVE* HIM, ARTHUR — A LOVE THAT *WE* NEVER FOUND.

BUT A *LOVE* YOU SEEMED TO FIND FOR *VIVIANNE!*

COME ON, WART. LET'S GET YOU OUT OF HERE BEFORE SOMETHING *STUPID* HAPPENS, EH?

VIVIANNE? I DON'T EVEN REMEMBER WHAT SHE *LOOKS* LIKE.

THAT IS, I SEEM TO RECALL . . .

WHY DIDN'T YOU *TELL* ME OF THIS? YOU COULD HAVE *TOLD ME* OF THIS!

WE WERE *MORE* THAN MAN AND WIFE; WE WERE *BEST FRIENDS!*

I WANTED TO, BUT I WAS TOO *SCARED!* IT WAS SO *WRONG* —

— YET AT THE SAME TIME FELT *SO RIGHT!*

ARGH! MY HEAD — *SPLITTING!*

ARTHUR! ARE YOU ALL RIGHT?

SPEAK TO ME! *WHAT'S HAPPENING?*

ARTHUR!

I — I REMEMBER IT ALL. . . .

"THIS IS MY REAL LIFE, VIVIANNE. AND TO LEAVE YOU – WILL TEAR MY HEART IN TWO."

KNOW THIS, LADY OF THE AKE. I WILL NEVER LOVE NOTHER AS I LOVE YOU."

I REMEMBER EVERYTHING!

"AND I WILL NEVER LOVE ANOTHER AS I LOVE YOU, ARTHUR AP UTHER PENDRAGON OF ALBION."

"ALL I WANT IS VIVIANNE. ALL I LOVE IS VIVIANNE. AND EVERY SECOND I'M AWAY FROM HER KILLS ME THAT LITTLE PIECE MORE."

"REMOVE MY MEMORIES OF MY LOVE FOR THE LADY OF THE LAKE."

I LOVED ER. AND THEN I FORGOT HER.

THIS WAS YOUR WORK, WIZARD! YOU TOOK THESE FROM ME!

I DID, MY KING –

– BECAUSE YOU BEGGED ME TO. AND I COULDN'T REVERSE THE SPELL.

I BEGGED YOU? TO FORGET *VIVIANNE*? TO FORGET *THIS*?

AND YOU *LET* ME? YOU AGREED FOR ME TO WALK *BLINDLY INTO BETRAYAL*? THEN WHY *NOW* REMIND ME?

I DIDN'T. YOUR SUBCONSCIOUS DID, BECAUSE YOU *NEEDED* TO REMEMBER. YOU NEEDED TO REMEMBER THAT GUINEVERE *WASN'T* YOUR FIRST LOVE. THAT YOU TOO LOVED *ANOTHER* AS SHE DOES.

AND YOU NEEDED TO REMEMBER FOR *HIM*.

IT HAS BEEN A *YEAR AND A DAY* IN AVALON, SIR GAWAIN.

ARE YOU READY TO UPHOLD *YOUR END* OF THE BARGAIN?

SIR BERTILAK. I DIDN'T *KNOW* ABOUT THE GLAMOUR! HE THOUGHT I WAS UNCARING AND RUDE TO VIVIANNE!

AND IT WAS *TRUE!* BUT GAWAIN CANNOT DIE FOR *MY* SINS!

I WILL **HONOR** OUR BARGAIN, SIR KNIGHT. ALTHOUGH IT GIVES ME NO **PLEASURE** TO DIE THIS DAY.

I HAVE TO **STOP** THIS!

ARTHUR, **PLEASE!**

TO TAKE ON THE GREEN KNIGHT IS **SUICIDE!** AS MERLIN SAID, HE **WON'T KILL** GAWAIN!

AND WHAT IF HE **DOES?** WILL YOU GIVE ME ONE **MORE** REASON TO HATE LANCELOT, GUINEVERE? FOR **HE** SHOULD BE STANDING THERE! MY **CHAMPION!**

GAWAIN, YOU HAVE **DONE** YOUR PART. AND I HAVE DONE **MINE.**

LET ME AT LEAST **DIE** IN YOUR PLACE, TO DO THE ONE THING THAT I **SHOULD** HAVE DONE TODAY.

DON'T BE A **FOOL**, LANCELOT! GET ON YOUR HORSE AND **RIDE!**

ESCAPE! BEFORE ARTHUR **STOPS** YOU!

STRIKE **ME**, COUSIN. FOR I WAS CAMELOT'S CHAMPION THE NIGHT YOU ARRIVED, AND AS SUCH SHOULD HAVE BEEN THE ONE TO **STRIKE** THE BLOW.

BUT **I** STRUCK THE BLOW, GREEN KNIGHT! SO **STRIKE ME!**

IS *THIS* THE LOYALTY I DESERVE? THAT *BOTH* OF YOU ARE WILLING TO DIE WHEN ONLY *ONE* NEEDS TO?

YES, MY LORD. AND THERE ISN'T A KNIGHT HERE TODAY WHO *WOULDN'T* TAKE MY PLACE!

PLEASE, MY KING. LET ME AT LEAST DIE WITH *HONOR*, BE USEFUL ONE LAST TIME.

NO, LANCELOT. *THIS* ISN'T YOUR PLACE TO DIE. THIS IS *MY* BATTLE TO FIGHT.

GAWAIN, ATTEND ME. LANCELOT, *STAY.* IF I *SURVIVE* THIS, THEN WE SHALL SPEAK.

I REMEMBER *EVERYTHING* NOW, SIR BERTILAK. I HAD FORGOTTEN, BUT NOW IT'S BACK.

GAWAIN SHOULDN'T PAY FOR MY CRIMES. IT WAS *MY* SLIGHT TO VIVIANNE, NOT HIS.

AGREED, BUT THE BARGAIN MUST STILL BE *COMPLETE.* DO YOU TAKE THE MAN'S PLACE?

I DO. TODAY I REMEMBERED A LOVE I DISCARDED FOR *DUTY*, AND I CANNOT LIVE WITH THE HURT I CAUSED HER *BECAUSE* OF THIS.

BE KIND TO ME, BERTILAK. STRIKE *TRUE.*

I ALWAYS *DO*, MY LORD KING.

SHUNK!

WHERE ONCE I SAW A *BOY*, NOW I SEE A MAN.

YOU HAVE REGAINED YOUR LOST MEMORIES, AND YOUR DEBT IS FULFILLED.

YOU ARE THE *TRUE* KING ONCE MORE.

GATHER THE *SHARDS OF THE BLADE.* WE NEED TO RETURN IT TO ITS RIGHTFUL KEEPER.

MY LORD, YOU *CANNOT!* LET ME DO IT FOR YOU! YOUR CHAMPION IS NO MORE.

WHO BETTER THAN *ONE OF YOUR KNIGHTS?*

TOO LONG HAVE I LET *OTHERS* FIGHT MY BATTLES, GAWAIN. IT IS TIME TO FACE MY FOES IN PERSON.

AND YOU HAVE TAKEN MY PLACE *TOO MANY* TIMES ALREADY, MY FRIEND. IT IS TIME FOR YOU TO REST.

GUINEVERE, WE BOTH LOVE *OTHERS.* BUT WHILE I MADE MYSELF FORGET, YOU WERE FORCED TO *LIVE* WITH YOUR SECRET.

LANCELOT, I CANNOT HATE YOU FOR FOLLOWING WHERE *FATE* LED YOU, AS I MUST FOLLOW MYSELF. SO GO IN PEACE.

HEAR THIS! NOBODY SHALL TOUCH GUINEVERE OR LANCELOT! THEY ARE *BANISHED FROM CAMELOT* –

– BUT STILL *WELCOME IN ALBION!*

A GOOD CHOICE, ARTHUR.

FOR WE HAVE *PLANS* FOR LANCELOT.

AS THE LADY OF THE LAKE, **ALL** LAKES ARE YOUR PORTALS, VIVIANNE.

AND THEREFORE **ALL** LAKES WILL PASS THE **MESSAGE** I MUST GIVE TO YOU.

I'M—

—I'M SORRY.

I **LOVE** YOU. I ALWAYS HAVE. BUT FOR A TIME I NEEDED TO **FORGET** THIS.

BUT INSTEAD OF FORGETTING THE **LOVE** I HAD FOR YOU, I FORGOT **YOU** ENTIRELY.

IN THE END, MORGANA TRICKED ME. SHE SENT MY **GREATEST LOVE** TO SEDUCE ME SO THAT SHE COULD CREATE A COPY OF ME—

—SO THAT SHE COULD CREATE **MORDRED.**

AT FIRST I DIDN'T UNDERSTAND WHY I SAW **YOU** THAT NIGHT, AND I STRUCK OUT. AT YOU, AT MY FRIENDS . . .

CALIBURN WAS DESTROYED BECAUSE OF MY STUPIDITY. MY FEARS. MY **COWARDICE.**

ALBION NO LONGER HAS A CHAMPION **WORTHY** ENOUGH TO WIELD THE BLADE. AND THEREFORE . . .

THAT'S A SHARD OF *CALIBURN?* THEN IT CAN'T BE USED!

ONLY THE PURE OF HEART OR *ARTHUR* CAN USE THE BLADE!

YOU FORGET ONE SMALL THING IN THE *FIFTEEN YEARS* YOU'VE TRAINED MORDRED, ULRIC –

– AND THAT IS THAT HE *IS* ARTHUR. IN EVERY MINUTE DETAIL. *OUR* ARTHUR.

IN TEN MORE YEARS HE WILL BE *READY.* AND IN ALBION ONLY *WEEKS* WILL HAVE PASSED.

ARTHUR IS WEAK. CONFUSED. *BROKEN.* AND WE WILL USE THIS TO DEFEAT HIM IN BATTLE.

BUT EVEN WITH A MAGIC SPEAR, I NEED AN *ARMY,* MOTHER.

WHERE WILL WE FIND THAT? FROM THE UNSEELIE COURT?

FROM THE *NORTHLANDS,* MY SON. HIRED HELP FROM THE FROZEN WASTES.

THE *SAXONS* WILL AID US. THEY OWE ULRIC A DEBT.

ARTHUR'S PEOPLE ARE LOST, FRACTURED. AND THEY WILL LOOK TO A *NEW* LEADER. A *BETTER, PURER* ARTHUR.

AND WITH YOUR MAGICAL SPEAR, *RHONGOMIANT,* YOU WILL *CLAIM* YOUR BIRTHRIGHT.

KILL ARTHUR. *REPLACE* ARTHUR.

BE ARTHUR.

CAMELOT.

WHAT DO I *DO,* MERLIN? HOW DO I *DEFEAT* MORGANA?

I THINK WE BOTH KNOW THAT THIS IS A BATTLE WE WON'T WALK AWAY FROM *ALIVE,* MY KING.

BUT NO MATTER WHAT, WE *MUST* STOP MORGANA AND THE UNSEELIE COURT.

THE REPORTS SAY THAT *SAXONS* ARE INVADING — THAT THEY HEAD FOR CAMELOT. IS THIS THE START?

IS THIS HOW IT ALL *ENDS?*

DEAR ECTOR, I DID INDEED. I RELEASE YOU ALL FROM YOUR *OATHS* TO ME.

WHAT?

I HAVE SPENT MY LIFE SEEING VISIONS OF MY *FUTURE,* AND THERE IS ONLY ONE SCENE I SEE. MY *DEATH.*

IT APPROACHES, AND I HAVE NO DESIRE TO CAUSE *YOUR* DEATHS IN THE PROCESS. SO TAKE MY LOVE AND LEAVE CAMELOT. BE *SAFE.*

IF YOU DECIDE TO STAY — TO STAND *WITH* ME — THEN DRINK WITH ME FROM THIS MOST *HOLY OF GRAILS,* THE *CHALICE* GIVEN TO ME BY THE SEELIE COURT IN MY DARKEST HOUR.

BECOME MY BROTHERS *ONCE MORE* IN THIS MOST SOLEMN PACT.

I'VE LOOKED AFTER YOU ALL MY LIFE, WART. NO REASON TO STOP NOW.

UNTIL THE *VERY END.*

YOU'RE MY *SON,* ARTHUR — MORE SO THAN UTHER'S. I RAISED YOU.

AND I'LL BE DAMNED IF I *DESERT* YOU NOW. UNTIL THE END IT IS.

SOMEWHERE IN ALBION.

I DON'T *UNDERSTAND*, LANCELOT! WHY DO YOU HAVE TO DO THIS?

WHY DO YOU HAVE TO *LEAVE* ME?

BECAUSE THIS IS HOW IT HAS *TO BE.*

BECAUSE THIS IS HOW *MY STORY ENDS.*

COME, MY PRINCE. THE *UNSEELIE COURT* HAS NEED OF THEIR NEW *CHAMPION.*

I'M *SORRY*, MY LOVE. APOLOGIZE TO ARTHUR FOR ME.

THE UNSEELIE REALM, ARCADIA.

WONDERFUL! THE CHAMPION *FALLS!*

THE UNSEELIE COURT CANNOT FAIL!

I TOLD YOU THIS WOULD WORK!

NOW, LET US *END* THIS CHARADE!

WHAT OF YOU, *OTTA BIG-KNIFE?*

WILL YOUR SAXON SOLDIERS *FIGHT* FOR ME? WILL THEY FIGHT FOR *MORDRED?*

WHILE I LEAD THEM, MY SOLDIERS WILL FIGHT FOR *GOLD,* AND IF *YOU* ARE THE ONE GIVING US THIS GOLD—

—THEN WE WILL *FIGHT* FOR YOU.

CAMELOT.

HOW LONG HAVE YOU BEEN ABLE TO SPY INTO THE UNSEELIE REALM, SIR BERTILAK? MORE *FAERIE MAGICK?*

WE HAVE SOMEONE *HIDDEN* IN THE COURT. THEY ALLOW US ENTRY PAST THE *WARDINGS.* AND WHILE MORGANA PLOTS, SHE PAYS LITTLE ATTENTION.

SHE IS PREPARING HER MAGICIANS AND HER SOLDIERS FOR WAR, BUT THEY WILL BE *ARROGANT* AND *UNDISCIPLINED.*

ULRIC HAS SCANT TIME TO TRAIN THESE MERCENARIES TO HIS STYLE OF FIGHTING. IF WE STRIKE THEM *HARD,* THEY WILL FLEE.

IT WILL BE A BLOODY BATTLE, ARTHUR. AND IT WILL BEGIN SOON. *BE READY.*

THEY HAVE *NUMBERS,* BUT WE HAVE BETTER TACTICIANS. ECTOR AND BEDIVERE WILL—

WHAT'S GOING ON?

GOOD *MORNING,* MY KING.

I'VE COME TO *HELP* YOU AGAINST THE USURPER TO YOUR THRONE. I HOPE THAT'S ALL RIGHT?

GUINEVERE! WHAT ARE YOU *DOING!*

YOU BANISHED ME FROM CAMELOT, BUT NOT *ALBION.* AND SO I *FIGHT* FOR IT.

AS FOR LANCELOT, HE FIGHTS FOR *MORDRED.* THE UNSEELIE COURT MADE HIM THEIR CHAMPION.

SO IT'S TRUE. LANCELOT REALLY *DOES* BECOME MY ENEMY.

YES, MY KING. . . .

". . . LANCELOT IS A *HERO* NO LONGER."

IT'S *LANCELOT!* SOMEONE *HELP* HIM!

CAREFUL WITH HIM!

MERLIN NEVER SPOKE OF *THIS!* HE SAID YOU WOULD *SURVIVE!*

I AM OF... *FAERIE,* MY QUEEN. AND BY DOING THIS I... AM *PURE* ONCE MORE.

I WILL RETURN... IN *FAERIE* SPRING...

ARTHUR... I AM *SORRY...* FOR WHAT I DID...

SHUSH, OLD FRIEND. YOU FOLLOWED YOUR HEART, NOTHING MORE.

WE'LL GET YOU TO MERLIN. HE'LL SAVE YOU. JUST LIE BACK, SAVE YOUR STRENGTH.

YOU SPOKE TO MERLIN?

THIS WAS HIS PLAN. TO *CONVINCE* MORGANA THAT LANCELOT HAD FINALLY TURNED UNSEELIE.

TO STRIKE AT THE HEAD OF THE SNAKE. TO BREAK THEM BEFORE THEY EVEN HIT US. WITH ULRIC *GONE,* THE SAXONS WON'T BE AS LOYAL.

WE KNEW WE'D HAVE DIFFICULTIES KILLING *MORDRED.* MORGANA HAS HIM MAGICALLY WARDED. ONLY A WEAPON LIKE *EXCALIBUR* WILL PASS HER SPELLS.

BUT WE *COULD* KILL ULRIC. I JUST NEVER EXPECTED IT TO END LIKE THIS.

—KAFF—

MERLIN! WHAT HAPPENED?

I *BURNED AWAY* MORGANA'S UNSEELIE TAINT, NIMUE.

WITH IT GONE, SHE'S AS SHE WAS. AND WE WERE *EVICTED* FROM THE UNSEELIE REALM.

WIZARD, I CAN THINK *CLEARLY* FOR THE FIRST TIME IN —*HNF*— *YEARS.*

I *REGRET*— KAFF— SO MUCH. BUT I... *FORGIVE YOU....*

COME ON! THESE ARE JUST *BURNS!* WE CAN HEAL THESE!

I AM SO SORRY, MY LOVE, BUT *NOTHING* CAN —*HNG*— HEAL *THESE* WOUNDS.

I USED MY *LIFE'S ENERGY* TO BURN THE GLAMOUR AWAY. I'M *DYING.*

YOU CAN'T DIE. I WON'T *LET* YOU.

I'M A *DRYAD*—A TREE SPRITE. I CAN PROTECT YOU, *HOLD* YOU, GIVE YOU THE TIME NEEDED TO GAIN YOUR STRENGTH.

LITTLE BY LITTLE, NO MATTER HOW MANY YEARS, OR EVEN *CENTURIES* IT TAKES TO HEAL YOU.

I *LOVE* YOU, MERLIN AMBROSIUS. NOW *KISS* ME.

YOU CAME TO ME AFTER I *BANISHED* YOU.

YOU *FOUGHT* FOR ME EVEN AFTER I *FORBADE* YOU.

THEY WILL FOLLOW YOU, BECAUSE THEY SEE IN YOU WHAT I DO. *THE QUEEN OF THE BRITONS.*

WE ALL FOLLOWED OUR HEARTS, AND WE ALL LOST. LANCELOT IS *DEAD.* AND YOU — NNG — HOPE FOR A *MIRACLE* IN SPRING.

WAIT FOR HIM . . . IN *CAMELOT.* MY KNIGHTS WILL ADVISE YOU. . . . NEVER HAVE I BEEN *PROUDER* OF THEM.

BEDIVERE, COME CLOSER. . . . I HAVE A . . . *TASK* FOR YOU.

ANYTHING, MY LORD.

TAKE *EXCALIBUR* TO THE LAKE, AND THROW IT IN.

BUT, MY LORD — IT IS YOUR *SWORD!*

NO . . . IT IS THE LADY OF THE LAKE'S . . . PROPERTY . . .

RETURN IT TO VIVIANNE. . . . *APOLOGIZE* FOR MY ABSENCE. . . .

TELL HER . . . I NEED TO . . . *SLEEP* FOR A MOMENT. . . .

I JUST . . . NEED TO . . . SLEEP . . .

NO, ARTHUR! *PLEASE!* STAY WITH US! *DON'T LEAVE US!*

HE'S GONE.

WE NEED TO START LOOKING FOR SURVIVORS.

IGNORE WHAT HE SAID. *YOU* MUST DECIDE WHICH OF YOU *RULES* NOW THAT HE IS GONE.

NO, MY QUEEN. ARTHUR SPOKE THE *TRUTH.* WE SAW YOU IN BATTLE TODAY.

YOU FOUGHT WITH US. YOU *BLED* WITH US. UNTIL CAMELOT FALLS, UNTIL THE VERY END . . .

. . . WE *PLEDGE OUR LIVES TO YOU.*

AND YOU CAN *ALL* STOP THAT *RIGHT NOW.*

YOU CAN SWEAR ALL THE OATHS AND PROMISES YOU WANT TO — *LATER.* BUT FIRST WE HAVE ONE LAST PROMISE TO KEEP.

WHAT'S THAT?

WE RETURN EXCALIBUR TO THE LADY OF THE LAKE.

WE TELL HER OF HER TRUE LOVE'S *DEATH.*

AND THEN WE *MOURN* TOGETHER.

THE LAKE.

BUT I'M JUST NOT SURE THAT *THIS* IS THE RIGHT COURSE OF ACTION!

THAT'S THE *THIRD TIME* YOU'VE SAID THAT.

JUST *THROW* THE DAMNED THING!

ALL RIGHT. BUT I *STILL* THINK WE SHOULD HAVE KEPT IT!

LADY OF THE LAKE! WE *RETURN YOUR SWORD!*

SPLASH!

I EXPECTED SOMETHING *BIGGER.*

COME, WE FULFILLED THE PROMISE. WE HAVE A *KINGDOM* TO REBUILD.

THE SAXONS WILL STILL NEED TO BE *STOPPED,* AND WE NEED TO FIND MERLIN, DISCOVER WHAT *HAPPENED* TO MORGANA—

EVERYONE! LOOK AT THE *WATER!*

ARTHUR GOES *HOME.*

AS SHOULD WE ALL. WE HAVE *DEAD* TO BURY...

...AND *HEROES* TO SING GREAT SONGS OF.

"BUT OF *KING ARTHUR* IS NO MORE KNOWN. SOME MEN, INDEED, SAY THAT HE IS *NOT* DEAD, BUT ABIDES IN THE HAPPY VALLEY OF *AVILION,* UNTIL SUCH TIME AS HIS COUNTRY'S NEED IS *SOREST,* WHEN HE SHALL COME AGAIN AND DELIVER IT."

"OTHERS SAY THAT, OF A TRUTH, HE *IS* DEAD, AND THAT, IN THE FAR WEST, HIS TOMB MAY BE SEEN, AND WRITTEN ON IT THESE WORDS:"

"*HERE LIES ARTHUR, ONCE KING AND KING TO BE.*"

LE MORTE D'ARTHUR, SIR THOMAS MALORY, 1485

END.

TONY LEE

Tony Lee has been a writer for more than twenty years. He started his career in games journalism, but moved into writing for radio, TV, and magazines.

In 2004 Tony turned his attention to comics writing and has since worked for a variety of publishers, including Marvel Comics, IDW Publishing, Markosia, Rebellion, Panini, and Titan.

He has contributed to many popular and high-profile properties such as *X-Men*, *Spider Man*, *Starship Troopers*, *Wallace & Gromit*, and *Shrek*.

He is currently the writer of the ongoing *Doctor Who* comic series for IDW Publishing.

In 2010 Tony became a New York Times #1 Best-Selling Graphic Novelist for his adaptation of *Pride & Prejudice & Zombies: The Graphic Novel*.

SAM HART

Sam Hart is a comic book artist and newspaper and magazine illustrator. He has worked on *Starship Troopers*, *Judge Dredd*, and *Hamlet* and for publishers Markosia, Oni Press, and DC Comics, amongst others. Born in England, he lives and teaches comic art in Brazil.

To Tracy, my Muse and Inspiration.
And Doreen Lee, the first and best editor
I ever had. Rest In Peace, Mum.
T. L.

To all my teachers ever, for the classes,
books and conversation.
And to Fabi.
S. H.

Copyright © 2011 by Tony Lee
Illustrations copyright © 2011 by Sam Hart

First U.S. edition 2011

Library of Congress Cataloging-in-Publication Data is available.

Library of Congress Catalog Card Number pending

ISBN 978-0-7636-4644-8 (hardcover)
ISBN 978-0-7636-4643-1 (paperback)

10 11 12 13 14 15 SWT 10 9 8 7 6 5 4 3 2 1

Printed in Dongguan, Guangdong, China

This book was typeset in Wild Words and Archetype.
The illustrations were created digitally.

Candlewick Press
99 Dover Street
Somerville, Massachusetts 02144

visit us at www.candlewick.com